NAKED MOLE RATS

Do Your Kids Know This?

A Children's Picture Book

Amazing Creature Series

Tanya Turner

PUBLISHED BY:

Tanya Turner

TABLE OF CONTENTS

Naked Mole Rats

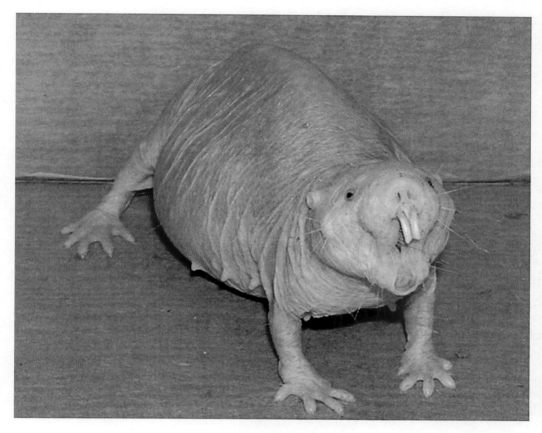

The Naked Mole Rat.
Image from Flickr by Jedimentat44.

The Naked Mole Rat is exactly what it sounds like – it's a species of rat belonging to the order of rodents, and it is called "naked" because it has very little hair, leaving its skin totally exposed.

This animal is also called by other names, such as Sand Puppy and Desert Mole Rat. If you've seen newly born puppies, then you know that they somewhat look like a mouse or a rat, which is why it's called a Sand Puppy. The sand part refers to the type of place they prefer to live in.

Its other name, Desert Mole Rat, is easier to understand. Of course, they can be found in deserts, and the very nature of the animal called a mole is that they live underground – just like Naked Mole Rats.

This animal is therefore very interesting because of its looks and its overall characteristics. Wouldn't you like to know it better?

Read on and you will find out how amazing Naked Mole Rats are.

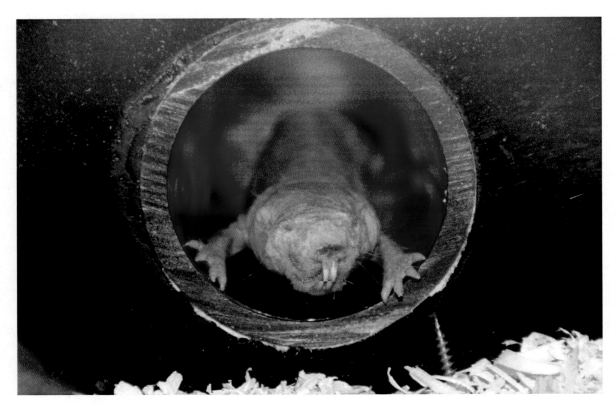

Naked Mole Rats use their teeth to dig underground tunnels.
Image from Shutterstock by belizar.

Getting to Know Naked Mole Rats

Naked Mole Rats are small animals – they are only about three to four inches long, just about the size of a regular species of rat. As for their weight, they only weigh around 1 to 1.2 ounces, which is quite light. The Queen, which is bigger than the rest of her colony, will also weigh slightly more.

This type of rat has very small eyes, and they have poor eye sight, too. As for their legs, these are thin and short. Their legs are also capable of moving forward and backward.

Another thing that you would immediately notice when you look at a Naked Mole Rat is its teeth. Their teeth are large, and they bulge from their mouth. Although they look strange because of their teeth, these are actually very useful to them because they use their teeth to dig through the ground.

Their lips are also sealed behind their teeth. The reason for this is to keep dirt from getting into their mouths as they dig through the ground.

Are they actually hairless? Well, they have very few strands of hair on their bodies, and because of this, their skin is exposed. They have wrinkled, pinkish or yellowish skin – which looks kind of awkward, as we are used to animals having hair or fur.

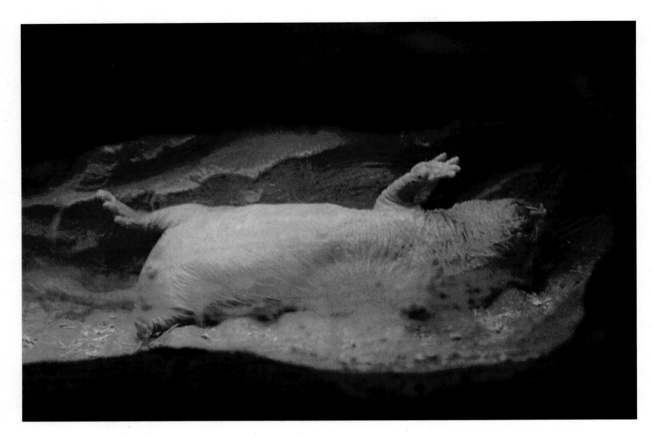

A sleeping Naked Mole Rat.
Image from Flickr by brx0.

Where Can You Find Naked Mole Rats?

Naked Mole Rats are mostly found in East Africa. They are in abundance in the grasslands of Ethiopia, Somalia, and Kenya.

They live in tunnels under the ground (which they themselves build). There can be about 80 individuals living as one group, called a colony.

Baby Naked Mole Rats.
Image from Flickr by Just chaos.

Understanding Male and Female Naked Mole Rats and Their Colonies

Naked Mole Rats are mammals, not insects. However, they also live in colonies (or groups) similar to bees and ants, with about 20 to 300 individuals per colony. Like said insects, they also have a Queen.

The Queen, which is the female reproducing Naked Mole Rat, is the most important of all the members of a colony. Typically, there is only one Queen per colony. Another female reproducing Naked Mole Rat will only replace the current Queen when it dies.

Note that Queen Naked Mole Rats are bigger than nonproducing males and females. In fact, they are even larger than reproducing males (the males that mate with the Queen).

A Queen Naked Mole Rat and its baby.
Image from Shutterstock by belizar.

What's really interesting about the Queens is that they usually start out as non-reproducing females (since there can only be one Queen per colony). But when the Queen of the colony dies, a regular non-reproducing female will suddenly increase in size to take over the role of the Queen. Its body will stretch out, its backbone will stretch out, too. Aside from being physically bigger, it will also be capable of reproducing baby Naked Mole Rats. In situations when there are many females that want to assume the role of Queen, they will fight among themselves and the winner will become the Queen.

Next to the Queen, the reproducing males are the next important members of the colony – and there can be a lot of them in a group (about three per colony). Their main role in the colony is to mate with the Queen.

A group of Naked Mole Rats sleeping in their tunnel.
Image from Shutterstock by bimserd.

Like ants, there are also worker Naked Mole Rats. As workers, they can't mate with the Queen (they are actually sterile, meaning they are not capable of making a female pregnant). The main role of workers is to take care of the other members of the colony.

They are in charge of providing food for the colony and they are tasked with cleaning duties around the colony. If there are newborn Naked Mole Rats, they also need to take care of them. The Queen will only tend to her offspring for a while and the workers will eventually take over in feeding, grooming, protecting, and warming them.

Worker Naked Mole Rats that are a little bigger than the others can also serve as the soldiers of the colony. They are the ones that are in charge of protecting their colony in case of attacks from other animals.

Diet

As underground creatures, the diet of Naked Mole Rats is mainly comprised of tubers. Tubers refer to stems and plant crops that grow under the ground. These are actually good sources of food, as they can depend on them for a long time. Naked Mole Rats only eat the insides of the tubers – and because of this, the remaining outside part can regrow into new ones.

Naked Mole Rats build their homes underground.
Image from Shutterstock by poeticpenguin.

Breeding and Reproduction

A one-year-old Queen is already ready for breeding. In the wild, Naked Mole Rats are known to breed about once a year. However, in captivity (such as when they are kept in zoos), they have been known to breed more frequently. Sometimes, they can even breed every 80 days. Eighty days is really quite short, especially when you consider that it takes 70 days for them to give birth.

Naked Mole Rats give birth to three to 12 baby Naked Mole Rats called pups. These pups are born blind and are really small – weighing only about .07 ounces.

When it's cold, Naked Mole Rats stay close to one another.
Image from Shutterstock by poeticpenguin.

A Closer Look at Naked Mole Rats

Naked Mole Rats are mammals (just like humans). As such, they need oxygen to breathe. However, the supply of oxygen is very limited underground, since oxygen is present in the air. So how does the Naked Mole Rat survive?

Well, their bodies have adjusted to having little oxygen. Their lungs are actually small and their breathing pattern is slower than other animals (and humans). In fact, their breathing pattern is even slower than that of a mouse, which is a close relative.

The bodies of Naked Mole Rats can also tolerate long periods of being hungry. Because of this, they won't easily starve to death when there's a limited supply of food. Their bodies will adapt to the situation by slowing down its metabolism by about 25%, so that it can conserve its energy consumption and continue to live, in spite of being hungry.

Naked Mole Rats have wrinkled skin.
Image from Shutterstock by Taylorbear.

Regulation of Body Temperature

Mammals (such as humans) are able to automatically regulate their body temperature in order to survive extremely hot and cold situations. In such cases, our bodies won't easily break down, unless the situation is really serious.

Know that it's not that way with Naked Mole Rats – their bodies can't easily adjust to too much cold and too much heat – and they can easily die because of this. However, they have evolved to compensate this lack of regulation and are able to survive despite this.

Naked Mole Rats live in colonies.
Image from Wikimedia Commons by Benny Mazur.

When Naked Mole Rats sense cold, they will keep themselves warm by staying close to one another. This way, their body heat will be more contained and they will feel less cold. In some cases, they will climb up their underground tunnels so as to stay closer to the surface of the ground. The temperature is colder in the deeper parts of their underground tunnel. However, it's a little warmer near the surface of the ground if the sun is shining.

If the weather becomes too hot for them, they also know how to deal with this. They will simply position themselves deeper in their underground tunnel, as the environment is colder down there.

Naked Mole Rats have very few strands of hair on their bodies.
Image from Wikimedia Commons by wikimedia de.User Einer_flog_zu_Weit.

Sensitivity to Pain

Humans have a component called Substance P in their skin, which allows us to feel pain. Go ahead and pinch yourself – do you feel pain? That's because you have Substance P in your skin. Because of Substance P, the feeling of pain is transferred through the nerves to the brain, and we can therefore respond to it.

Note that Naked Mole Rats don't have Substance P in their skin, so, they can't feel pain on their skin. In fact, scientists have found that they don't even feel pain when exposed to acid and capsaicin. Human skin (and other animals' skin, for that matter) will literally burn from acid exposure and feel the pain. Capsaicin, which is the main component of chili peppers, will also cause discomfort and irritation on the skin.

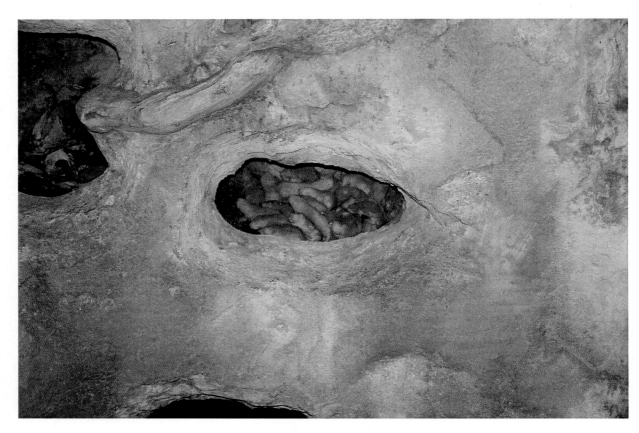

Baby Naked Mole Rats are called pups.
Image from Wikimedia Commons by Edward Russell.

When Naked Mole Rats are exposed to acid and Capsaicin, they don't have any reaction. Their skin will still burn when acid comes into contact with their skin, but they won't feel any kind of pain. As can be expected, they also won't feel any irritation when they come into contact with Capsaicin.

Scientists have even experimented with them and injected some subjects with Substance P. And you know what happened? The Naked Mole Rats became sensitive to Capsaicin and their skin became irritated. Still, they didn't have any reaction to acid, which is a really strong element. This only goes to show that Naked Mole Rats are not sensitive to pain – that even if Substance P is artificially injected in them, their tolerance for pain is still very high.

Naked Mole Rats are not sensitive to pain.
Image from Wikimedia Commons by Ltshears.

Nature has actually designed Naked Mole Rats with the special ability of being insensitive to pain. Since they basically live underground where the presence of carbon dioxide is high, acid can build up inside their bodies and destroy their tissues. Carbon dioxide poisoning can kill animals (and even people). Since an enclosed space can cause the level of carbon dioxide to increase, it is the normal environment of Naked Mole Rats.

Another advantage to having no Substance P in their bodies is that Naked Mole Rats are free from other skin discomforts. They don't even feel itchy, so they don't need to scratch those itchy spots like most animals do (and humans, too, right?).

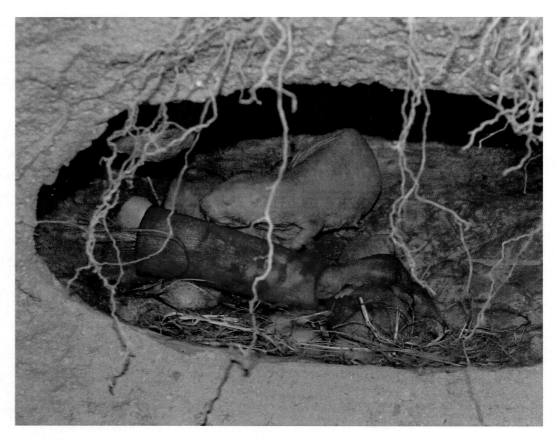

Naked Mole Rats eating carrots.
Image from Wikimedia Commons by Ltshears.

Life Span

Naked Mole Rats have long lives, as they can live to about 31 years. That's already considered a long time for animals and even among rodents. In fact, they are considered to be the longest living type of rodent. Compared to mice, which can only live to about three years, you will agree that they really do have a long life span.

What makes them long-lived? Well, for one, they have been known to be unaffected by the killer disease called cancer. Cancer is a deadly disease, and it has shortened the lives of animals and humans alike. However, this disease doesn't affect Naked Mole Rats, so that's one less disease that can kill them.

You already know about their insensitivity to pain. This, too, is a big factor in their lifespan. Know that the body also goes through a period of stress when it experiences pain – and exposure to stress can bring about (and worsen) diseases.

Remember their ability to slow down their metabolism when there's a shortage in food supply? That helps in preserving their lives, too. Aside from not immediately dying from hunger, it also prevents damages in their system. Such a characteristic can also slow down their aging process.

Naked Mole Rats can live up to about 31 years.
Image from Wikimedia Commons by Momotarou2012.

Life Span

While the Queen Naked Mole Rat can only live for about 13 to 18 years, other members of the colony can live up to about 31 years.

Status

Naked Mole Rats are far from being extinct. They are even far from being labeled as an endangered species because there are just too many of them. Their population is widespread in Africa. Because of their relatively short gestational period and ability to give birth to multiple pups at a time, they are able to reproduce more quickly than the older generations die off.

An animated picture of a Naked Mole Rat.
Image from Shutterstock by Lorelyn Medina.

Naked Mole Rats as Pets

Know that it's not very practical to keep Naked Mole Rats as pets. Yes, they're interesting and some even consider them cute. Consider their lifestyle – they mostly live underground – and it's hard to successfully create an environment where they can live in such a setting.

Made in the USA
San Bernardino, CA
19 August 2019